MW01471015

OVERCOMING ADVERSITY:
SHARING THE AMERICAN DREAM

HALLE BERRY

MASON CREST PUBLISHERS
PHILADELPHIA

OVERCOMING ADVERSITY:
SHARING THE AMERICAN DREAM

Charles Barkley
Halle Berry
Cesar Chavez
Kenny Chesney
George Clooney
Johnny Depp
Tony Dungy
Jermaine Dupri
Jennifer Garner
Kevin Garnett
John B. Herrington
Salma Hayek
Vanessa Hudgens
Samuel L. Jackson

Norah Jones
Martin Lawrence
Bruce Lee
Eva Longoria
Malcolm X
Carlos Mencia
Chuck Norris
Barack Obama
Rosa Parks
Bill Richardson
Russell Simmons
Carrie Underwood
Modern American
  Indian Leaders

**OVERCOMING ADVERSITY:
SHARING THE AMERICAN DREAM**

HALLE BERRY

MAURENE J. HINDS

**MASON CREST PUBLISHERS
PHILADELPHIA**

ABOUT CROSS-CURRENTS

When you see this logo, turn to the Cross-Currents section at the back of the book. The Cross-Currents features explore connections between people, places, events, and ideas.

Produced by OTTN Publishing, Stockton, New Jersey

Mason Crest Publishers
370 Reed Road
Broomall, PA 19008
www.masoncrest.com

Copyright © 2009 by Mason Crest Publishers. All rights reserved.
Printed and bound in the United States of America.

First printing

1 3 5 7 9 8 6 4 2

Library of Congress Cataloging-in-Publication Data

  Hinds, Maurene J.
   Halle Berry / Maurene J. Hinds.
     p. cm. — (Sharing the American dream : overcoming adversity)
  Includes bibliographical references.
  ISBN 978-1-4222-0596-9 (hardcover) — ISBN 978-1-4222-0738-3 (pbk.)
 1. Berry, Halle—-Motion picture actors and actresses—United States—Biography—Juvenile literature. 2. African American motion picture actors and actresses—Biography—Juvenile literature. I. Title.
  PN2287.B4377 H56 2008
  791.4302/8092B 22
                            2008024456

OVERCOMING ADVERSITY: SHARING THE AMERICAN DREAM

TABLE OF CONTENTS

Chapter One: A Door Has Been Opened	**6**
Chapter Two: Model Student	**13**
Chapter Three: "Hallewood"	**20**
Chapter Four: Oscar to X-Men	**28**
Chapter Five: A New Chapter	**36**
Cross-Currents	**42**
Chronology	**52**
Accomplishments/Awards	**54**
Further Reading	**56**
Internet Resources	**57**
Glossary	**58**
Chapter Notes	**59**
Index	**62**

CHAPTER ONE

A DOOR HAS BEEN OPENED

Five movies. Five actresses. One winner. The crowd at the Kodak Theatre in Hollywood, California, quieted after watching the last movie clip. Suspense hung in the air. Five actresses were nominated in the Best Actress category at the 74th Annual Academy Awards. Halle Berry, Judi Dench, Nicole Kidman, Sissy Spacek, and Renée Zellweger waited as presenter Russell Crowe opened the envelope. "And the Oscar goes to . . . Halle Berry."

An obviously shocked Halle Berry stood, with her mother and husband at her side. She made her way to the stage to accept the award. "This moment is so much bigger than me," Halle said, fighting back tears. "This moment is for Dorothy Dandridge, Lena Horne, Diahann Carroll. It's for the women that stand beside me, Jada Pinkett, Angela Bassett, Vivica Fox. And it's for every nameless, faceless woman of color that now has a

> **READ MORE**
>
> The 74th Annual Academy Awards were a landmark for African Americans on the screen. In addition to Halle Berry, two black actors took home awards. For details, see page 42.

A Door Has Been Opened   7

Making history: Halle Berry during her emotional acceptance speech after winning Best Actress honors at the 74th Academy Awards, March 24, 2002. It was the first time an African American had been awarded the Oscar for Best Actress in a leading role.

chance because this door tonight has been opened. Thank you. I'm so honored. I'm so honored."

Making History

On March 24, 2002, Halle Berry became the first African American to win an Academy Award for Best Actress in a leading role. Many people believed this milestone was long overdue.

Over the years, Hollywood has largely reflected American society and its prevailing attitudes. From the 1920s through the 1950s, there were few good roles for black actors; the parts that were available tended to portray African Americans in offensive stereotypes or were minor roles. During this period, blacks suffered discrimination in American society at large. In the South, a system of laws and practices known as Jim Crow kept blacks from using the same public facilities as whites. Blacks couldn't go to the same schools, eat at the same restaurants, stay at the same hotels, drink from the same water fountains, or use the same public restrooms as whites.

Dorothy Dandridge, whom Halle Berry mentioned in her Oscar acceptance speech—and whom she had portrayed in a 1999 movie—knew the racism of American society. Beautiful and talented, the African American Dandridge won small parts in Hollywood movies beginning in the late 1930s. By the early 1950s she had become an international singing star, and in 1954 she starred in *Carmen Jones*, an adaptation of the Georges Bizet opera *Carmen* with an all-black cast. Dandridge was nominated for a Best Actress Oscar for her portrayal of the title character. Yet despite

READ MORE
For a brief profile of the African American singer and actress Dorothy Dandridge, turn to page 44.

her success as a singer and an actress, she suffered discrimination because of her race. She was, for example, denied access to restrooms reserved for whites. While performing in Las Vegas, she was barred from using the hotel pool.

In the mid-1950s, around the time Dorothy Dandridge appeared in *Carmen Jones*, the civil rights movement began. Through protests, boycotts, and legal challenges, blacks struggled to win equality in American society. By the mid-1960s, major victories had been won. Jim Crow was dismantled, and the U.S. Congress enacted landmark civil rights legislation.

Dorothy Dandridge, circa 1955. The African American singer and actress garnered an Academy Award nomination for the title role in 1954's *Carmen Jones*. Despite this, she found it difficult to get good movie parts in color-conscious Hollywood.

This progress, however, didn't mean the end of prejudice against blacks. Laws can forbid discrimination, but they can't change attitudes overnight.

Still, during the last three decades of the 20th century, African Americans made steady gains in a variety of fields. Yet popular culture didn't always keep pace. Black actors continued to find that relatively few good leading roles were available to them. This was reflected in the dearth of Academy Awards for African Americans. Between 1965 and 2001, in fact, no blacks won an Oscar in the Best Actor or Best Actress category—though Denzel Washington took home a Best Supporting Actor award in 1990, and Whoopi Goldberg was picked as Best Supporting Actress the following year.

> **READ MORE**
>
> As of 2008, Halle Berry was the only African American to win an Academy Award in the Best Actress category, but several African Americans have been honored as Best Actress in a Supporting Role. See page 46 for details.

One for Dorothy

In 1999, Halle Berry played a wonderful leading role—as Dorothy Dandridge in a film for the cable channel HBO. *Introducing Dorothy Dandridge* was very much a labor of love for Halle. She had worked to bring Dandridge's story to viewers for five long years, as a producer of the project.

Halle could relate to Dorothy Dandridge, the first African American nominated for a Best Actress Academy Award. The two were born in the same hospital in Cleveland, both struggled in Hollywood because of their skin color, and both had their share of personal heartache.

Halle felt connected to Dandridge in other ways as well. In the movie, for example, she wore one of Dandridge's gowns, and it fit her perfectly. Halle saw this as a sign that she had been on the right path in working so long and hard to get the movie into production. "It felt like validation," Halle said of first trying on the gown.

In a 1999 interview with *Ebony* magazine, Halle also described some unusual events surrounding the gown. During the making of the film, Halle said she heard noises in the closet where she kept Dandridge's gown. When she looked for the source of the sound, she saw a small dress floating in front of the gown. Was this Dorothy Dandridge's spirit visiting her? Halle

A Door Has Been Opened   11

Halle Berry backstage with her Oscar at the 74th Academy Awards.

was frightened, and she called one of Dandridge's close friends, who told her that if Dandridge's spirit was indeed visiting, she meant no harm. Halle decided that it was time for her to return the gown.

When *Introducing Dorothy Dandridge* premiered, on August 21, 1999, critics raved about Halle's performance. She eventually won an Emmy and a Golden Globe award for her portrayal of the actress.

Paving the Way

By 2000, after roles in the comic-book-inspired *X-Men* and the thriller *Swordfish*, Halle Berry had established herself as one of the top-earning actresses in her profession. Then Halle appeared in the movie for which she would win the Oscar: *Monster's Ball*. It was a gritty, decidedly unglamorous film, and she'd had to fight for her part because the producer thought she was too pretty for the role. Halle had also taken a huge pay cut to be in *Monster's Ball*.

Halle's persistence and financial sacrifice were vindicated when the Academy of Motion Picture Arts and Sciences honored her with a Best Actress Oscar. The award was also, in a sense, vindication for the African American performers Halle named in her acceptance speech, including Dorothy Dandridge, Lena Horne, and Diahann Carroll, who had perhaps not gotten the opportunities or the honors their talent merited. They had paved the way for Halle, and now Halle hoped her critical and box office success would open doors for other African American actresses who aspired to play leading roles in Hollywood films.

CHAPTER TWO

MODEL STUDENT

Halle Maria Berry was born in Cleveland, Ohio, on August 14, 1966. She was named after the Halle Brothers department store. Her mother, Judith Hawkins, had walked by the store when she was pregnant, and she thought that "Halle" sounded like a nice name.

A Troubled Union

Halle's father, Jerome Berry, was an African American. Her mother was a white woman from England. Halle did not know many of her relatives. Her mother's family had disowned Judith when she married Jerome. Biracial marriages were not as accepted in the 1960s as they later became. Halle never knew her father's side of the family.

The relationship between Halle's parents was a stormy one. Halle has said in several interviews that her father was an abusive alcoholic. "He beat my mom and my sister," Halle said in a 2002 interview with the *New York Times*. "He threw our dog against the wall. He never hit me. I felt a lot of guilt. When my sister saw him hitting my mother, she would jump in and get hit, but I would run and hide. I'd get out of the way."

The actress with her mother, Judith Hawkins Berry, who raised Halle and her older sister, Heidi, as a single mother.

True to Herself

When Halle was four, Jerome Berry left the family. Judith, a nurse, raised Halle and Heidi on her own. Judith moved her family from an inner-city neighborhood to Bedford, a mostly white suburb of Cleveland.

Other kids asked Halle why her mother was white. Halle did not understand why she looked different from her mother, or why people asked her mom if Halle and her sister were adopted. These experiences left her confused about her identity. Halle remembered that she and her sister were called names such as "Oreo" and "zebra." Halle's mother explained that, because her skin was darker, others would see her as an African American,

Model Student

not as a white or biracial person. "She taught me when I was little that I'm her daughter, I'm half white, but when you leave this house people will assume you're black and you'll be discriminated against," Halle recalled many years later. "So accept being black, embrace it. She said if I fight it, I will have a battle with them and a battle inside myself."

Halle took the lesson to heart. As her mother had urged, she embraced her African American ethnicity.

Proving Herself

Halle attended white schools, where she worked hard to prove herself and to be accepted. She threw herself into many activities. And she succeeded in just about everything she tried.

In high school, Halle was—in addition to being an excellent student—the head cheerleader, editor of the school paper, and class president. However, she did face some stumbling blocks. "I never did high-school plays," Halle recalled in a 2001 interview, "mainly because I went to an all-white high school and black kids didn't usually get cast in that kind of stuff. . . . Juliet can't be black! It was very limited in what we could do."

A view of downtown Cleveland. Halle Berry lived in the city until her mother moved the family to the suburb of Bedford, Ohio.

Halle Berry

More disturbing was Halle's experience as prom queen, which she recounted in a 2001 *New York Times* interview:

> I was the head cheerleader and president of the class. . . . I ran for prom queen and won, but they accused me of stuffing the ballot box. They said we had to flip a coin to determine who the prom queen really was. I picked heads and I won again. . . . But that experience stuck with me. I could be president and head cheerleader, but they were white and I was black and I was different. I realized that I always have to keep fighting.

American Beauty

After graduating from Bedford High School, Halle enrolled in Cuyahoga Community College, located in Cleveland. She planned

Halle Berry was head cheerleader at Bedford High School, as well as class president and editor of the school newspaper. Nevertheless, when she was elected prom queen, Halle faced accusations by white students that she had stuffed the ballot box.

on a career in journalism and got an internship with a local television station. However, Halle had trouble interviewing people. She was uncomfortable asking personal questions.

Halle's career plans soon took a turn. When she was 17, a boyfriend had submitted—without telling Halle—an application for her to enter a beauty contest. The application was accepted. Since winners received money for college, Halle decided to go ahead and participate in the contest. She won the title of Miss Teen Ohio, then went on to win the national pageant. She was crowned Miss Teen All American in 1985. The following year, she was first runner-up in the Miss USA pageant. She competed at the Miss World pageant in London in 1986, placing sixth.

In a 1995 interview with the *New York Times*, Halle described the importance of her beauty pageant experience. "Pageants teach you how to lose," she said, "and not be devastated. . . . It was great preparation for Hollywood."

Buoyed by her success in beauty pageants, Halle pursued a career in modeling. She also took acting classes and worked as a waitress to pay her bills. Her first experiences living on her own were not glamorous. She moved to Chicago and shared an apartment. When her roommate left her with a $1,300 rent bill, Halle asked her mom for $50 to buy food. Judith Berry refused. She told Halle that it had been her choice to live in the big city, and that she needed to learn what the real world was like. This experience, though difficult, helped Halle become more independent—and more determined to succeed.

A Turn on TV

In 1989 Halle moved to New York City to pursue an acting career. A talent agent named Vincent Cirrincione was looking for a beautiful African American actress to audition for a part on the daytime drama *Days of Our Lives*. One of Cirrincione's clients suggested

Cast members of the short-lived TV series *Living Dolls*. Clockwise from top left: Alison Elliott, Halle Berry, Michael Learned, Leah Remini, Deborah Tucker.

Halle. She didn't get that part, but with the help of Cirrincione—who would become her longtime manager—Halle landed a leading role in a TV sitcom called *Living Dolls*. The show was about a modeling representative (played by veteran actress Michael Learned) who shares a house with her aspiring young clients. Halle played one of the young models.

Living Dolls would flop—it ran for only a dozen episodes in 1989—but Halle had a life-changing experience while working on the show: she collapsed on the set during filming of an episode. Awakening in a hospital many hours later, Halle was told she had type 2 diabetes.

Type 2 diabetes is a serious medical condition that affects the body's ability to regulate sugar levels in the blood. Halle needed to learn how to manage her diabetes by checking her blood sugar levels regularly, eating a healthy diet, exercising, avoiding excessive stress, and, when necessary, using insulin.

She didn't find this easy. "It took five years," Halle recalled in a 2003 interview, "but I finally got [my diabetes] under control."

In the meantime, Halle was intent on advancing her career. In 1991 she had a recurring role in the prime-time soap opera *Knots Landing*. Halle's performance on *Knots Landing* caught the attention of a major film director, paving the way for her move to the big screen.

> **READ MORE**
> To find out more about diabetes, the serious medical disorder that Halle Berry lives with, turn to page 47.

CHAPTER THREE

"HALLEWOOD"

In 1991 Spike Lee, an acclaimed young movie director, was casting for his new film, *Jungle Fever*, when he saw Halle Berry on *Knots Landing*. Lee invited Halle to audition for a part.

Jungle Fever concerns a married black architect who has an affair with a white secretary. Lee wanted Halle to play the part of the architect's pretty wife. She surprised the director by asking him to let her read for another role: as a crack cocaine addict. "I liked that part better," Halle explained in 2001. "She was so screwed up. I could relate to that. She knows her beauty has swung the doors open, but she's also smart enough to realize that beauty has its limitations."

Lee was skeptical. He believed that Halle was too pretty for the part, but in the end she convinced him.

Role Research

Having had a middle-class suburban upbringing, Halle was unfamiliar with inner-city drug culture. She did extensive research to prepare herself for her role in *Jungle Fever*. Costar Samuel L. Jackson took her to areas of New York City where drug use was widespread. She interviewed dozens of recovering cocaine addicts. She also did something rather extraordinary.

"Hallewood" 21

"I went to a crack house," she recalled in 2003, "a real crack house. . . . When the policeman put the bulletproof vest on me, I should have said, 'OK, this is ridiculous.' Looking back now, I think I was crazy, but I didn't know anything about drugs, so I really had to go see it."

Halle Berry with director Spike Lee during filming of *Jungle Fever*, 1991. Lee had initially been reluctant to cast Halle in the role of crack addict Vivian, believing her to be too beautiful. But Halle's perseverance eventually persuaded him.

Halle's extensive research and commitment paid off. Her role in 1991's *Jungle Fever* was small, but critics took note of the 23-year-old actress.

Not Willing to Be Typecast

Halle and her manager, Vincent Cirrincione, pressed producers to consider her for roles that weren't specifically written for a black woman. A few such parts came her way. In *The Last Boy Scout*, an extremely violent 1991 action-mystery movie, Halle played a stripper opposite Bruce Willis and Damon Wayans. In 1994's *The Flintstones*, a live-action movie based on the old TV cartoon series, Halle was a conniving secretary. In *Executive Decision* (1996), she played a resourceful flight attendant aboard a hijacked airliner.

But choice roles were elusive, in part because of racial considerations. Even if a role had nothing to do with race, many producers were hesitant to "go black," fearing that audiences wouldn't see past the actor's skin color. "Some [film] executive explained it to me by talking about milk," Halle's manager, Vincent Cirrincione, noted. "They said milk is milk until you add a little Hershey."

Halle found the situation frustrating. "I want the same shot as everyone else," she told the *New York Times* in 1995. "But I never even got the chance to read for 'Silence of the Lambs' or 'Intersection' or 'Indecent Proposal.' The excuse is that a black woman would change what the movie was all about."

Halle continually encountered another obstacle when she sought to play tough, complex characters: her stunning beauty. Many people would be only too happy to have such a problem. But Halle was determined to challenge herself and master her craft. And she constantly found herself bumping up against producers and directors who assumed she wouldn't be right for roles that weren't glamorous or sexy.

"Hallewood"

Halle Berry and Jessica Lange in a publicity photo for the 1995 drama *Losing Isaiah*. Halle played a crack addict who abandons her infant, reforms her life, and then fights to win custody of the boy, who has since been adopted by a white social worker (played by Lange) and her husband.

One lead role that Halle desperately wanted—but that filmmakers were disinclined to consider her for—was as Khaila Richards in the 1995 movie *Losing Isaiah*. Khaila is a homeless African American crack addict who abandons her baby near a dumpster. The infant is found by garbage collectors and adopted by a white social worker and her husband. Several years later, after going through rehabilitation for her addiction and beginning to put her life back together, Khaila discovers that the son she believes she has killed is in fact alive. She goes to court to get him back.

Producers had already cast two-time Academy Award winner Jessica Lange in the role of the social worker when Halle asked to be considered for the role of Khaila. "Frankly, we wondered if somebody as gorgeous as Halle would be believable as a crack addict," admitted Sherry Lansing, the head of Paramount Pictures. "She was exceptional in 'Jungle Fever,' but it was a small role and quite a few years ago. And we wanted to be sure she could hold her own against Jessica."

Director Stephen Gyllenhaal shared Lansing's reservations. But he agreed to give Halle a screen test, playing a scene in which Khaila confesses to her rehab counselor that she left her baby in the trash. "With every take," Gyllenhaal recalled, "Halle got stronger and stronger. She has such a reservoir of emotion. I was blown away."

Halle got the part, and her performance impressed film critics such as Janet Maslin. "Ms. Berry is the most gorgeous young actress in American films right now, Maslin noted, "and she tackles this role with impressive passion. When a performer can look like a beauty queen and persuade an audience to follow her anywhere, she's a real star."

Love and Loss

As Halle's career began to soar, however, her personal life spiraled down. Around 1991 she had been involved in a brief relationship with an actor (she refused to identify him further) who beat her so severely that she lost most of the hearing in one ear. Then, in 1992, Halle met baseball star David Justice, an outfielder for the Atlanta Braves. They had a whirlwind romance and were married on New Year's Day of 1993.

Cracks in the relationship soon emerged. The two had to deal with the pressures and time commitments of their respective high-profile careers. "I wasn't good at being a baseball wife,"

"Hallewood" 25

Halle Berry and her husband, David Justice, at a celebrity softball game, January 1996. Within three months, Halle would file for a divorce amid allegations of abuse.

Halle would later admit. "I was lonely and really depressed and I wasn't a sports fan. David wanted me at the games with the other wives, so I went, but I had never watched baseball before." There were other, even more serious, issues in the marriage. Halle would later say that Justice was physically abusive. The couple's breakup was very messy and very public, providing endless fodder for gossip columns and tabloid TV programs. Halle and Justice were divorced in 1997.

The disintegration of her marriage hit Halle hard. She would later admit that she flirted with the idea of committing suicide, but was stopped by the thought of how much that would hurt her mother. One thing Halle did—on the very day her divorce became final—was to call her father. Halle hadn't seen him since she was 10, when her parents had briefly attempted to reconcile. "I had to track him down because I hadn't talked with him in years," Halle recalled.

> I was filled with pain and rage. I got him on the phone and released all this anger. I released it. I told him how much he had hurt me by abandoning our family, by not being in my life when I was a child. At the end of the conversation, he said 'I'm sorry.'"

That apology, of course, could not make up for how Jerome Berry had blighted Halle's childhood through his abuse and abandonment. His failure to provide a father's love, Halle would come to believe, partially explained her unhealthy relationships with men.

Refocusing

While still reeling from her divorce, Halle had to keep a commitment to star in a film called B*A*P*S (standing for "Black

African Princesses"). At first she wondered how she would get through the filming. "It's a comedy," she told an interviewer, "and I wasn't feeling very funny, so I wasn't confident that I would be able to be in that space. But it turned out to be very therapeutic. I could laugh and be silly and let go of all that negative energy." Halle may have benefited from her work on *B*A*P*S*, but most critics thought the 1997 movie was terrible.

By contrast, the critics loved Halle's next film, *Bulworth* (1998), whose screenplay was nominated for an Academy Award. The movie concerned an aging, disillusioned politician (played by Warren Beatty) who decides finally to tell the truth about everything. Halle played his love interest. Despite its positive critical reception, the biting political comedy did not do well at the box office.

Halle had little time to fret about that, however. She was busy trying to bring *Introducing Dorothy Dandridge* to fruition. And she had found another offscreen love interest.

CHAPTER FOUR

OSCAR TO X-MEN

Halle Berry met up-and-coming R&B singer Eric Benét in 1997. Benét was trying to juggle the demands of his music career while raising his young daughter by himself after the tragic death of her mother in a car accident. He and Halle became friends, and soon a romance blossomed.

In 1999 Benét released his second album, *A Day in the Life*. It was a smash hit and went platinum. That same year, Halle had a huge success of her own, coproducing and starring in the critically acclaimed *Introducing Dorothy Dandridge*.

Not All Golden

Personally and professionally, Halle seemed to have everything going for her. Soon, however, she found herself in the middle of a tabloid scandal—and some legal trouble.

In February 2000, just a month after winning a Golden Globe for *Introducing Dorothy Dandridge,* Halle ran a stoplight while driving one night in Hollywood. Halle's car slammed into another vehicle. Instead of remaining at

READ MORE
For information about the Golden Globe awards, turn to page 48.

Oscar to X-Men 29

Halle Berry in *Introducing Dorothy Dandridge*. The film was very much a labor of love for Halle, who not only portrayed the title character but also served as coproducer.

the scene of the accident, as is required by law, Halle drove herself to a hospital. Twenty stitches were needed to close a gash in her forehead. A woman in the car Halle hit suffered a broken wrist. She quickly filed a lawsuit against Halle.

The Los Angeles district attorney, meanwhile, considered charging Halle with a felony offense (a serious crime) for the hit-and-run accident. Halle could have faced up to a year in jail if convicted. Halle insisted that she hadn't intentionally left the scene of the accident. She said that she had no memory of the crash, probably because of the head injury she had suffered. The district attorney apparently believed her. After an investigation that lasted more than six weeks, Halle was charged with a misdemeanor, or minor offense. In court, she pleaded no contest—meaning that she did not dispute the charge—and the judge ordered her to pay a $13,500 fine and perform 200 hours of community service.

Though it could have turned out much worse for Halle, the entire episode was still very painful. The tabloid papers were especially cruel, which perhaps shouldn't have come as a surprise. But Halle also found that people she'd considered friends weren't supportive. "People I thought I was very close to distanced themselves from me," she told an interviewer. "It was very subtle. No one put me down or belittled me. It was the things people didn't say. The support that wasn't offered. They were real happy to stay around when things were great, but when this happened, it was like I had the plague."

One person whose support and love remained unwavering was Eric Benét. In the depths of her anguish, as she waited to see whether the district attorney would charge her with a felony, Halle worried that Benét would abandon her, just as her father had abandoned her. He didn't. "As the weeks went by, I thought, 'Wow, he's still here,'" she recalled. "And not just loving me.

Halle Berry and R&B singer Eric Benét, March 2001. The two had gotten married two months earlier.

Loving me hard. He showed me when I was too weak to stand, he would hold me up. When I was too fragile to think he'd help me figure it out. When I was too scared to face another day, he'd be my rock."

In January 2001, Halle and Benét were married. Halle later adopted his daughter, India.

Of Mutants and Monsters

In the meantime, Halle's box office appeal had gotten even bigger. She shot to superstardom in *X-Men* (2000). The movie, based on a popular comic book series, revolves around a group of people whose genetic mutations have given them special powers. Halle played the character of Storm, a mutant woman who can control the weather.

X-Men was a big hit at the box office, but some critics dismissed it as shallow and insubstantial. And some fans of the comic book series believed that the movie had given Halle's character short shrift. She disagreed, defending both the movie and her character in an interview with *Ebony* magazine. "The mutants face many of the same obstacles that we do as African-Americans," she said. "They're struggling to find equality within a society of non-mutants who fear them out of ignorance. Storm reminds everyone that, if anything is to change, we have to educate people out of their ignorance. That's the substance of who Storm is for me."

In 2001 Halle played a role that was about as far away from a comic book superhero as one could imagine, in a film no one dismissed as insubstantial. The character was Leticia Musgrove, a struggling, embittered waitress whose husband is on death row for a murder. The movie was *Monster's Ball*.

The role of Leticia had to be played by an African American actress. But, as had been the case with *Jungle Fever* and *Losing Isaiah*, Halle's beauty worked against her landing the part. Halle got a meeting with *Monster's Ball* producer Lee Daniels to argue her case. "We met for lunch," Daniels recalled, "and to be honest, at first I didn't think she had the backbone for the part. I didn't think it was in her makeup, and I told her so."

Halle refused to accept that assessment. She argued forcefully that just because someone is attractive doesn't mean he or she cannot be trampled down by life. "Of course, she was right," Daniels later admitted. "I realized that I was holding her looks against her. The strength of character that Halle showed at lunch was the same strength Leticia needed, and it's what convinced me she could do the job."

In the movie, Halle starred opposite Billy Bob Thornton, who played Hank Grotowski, a racist prison guard who has

Oscar to X-Men

carried out the execution of Leticia's husband. When Hank meets Leticia, he does not know that she is the dead man's widow. The two—both of whom are desperate and even tortured souls—are drawn toward one another. Hank's feelings for Leticia lead him to question his racist past—yet the film turns out to be anything but a simple story of redemption.

Monster's Ball required Halle to play a very complex character, and she was up to the challenge. "Ms. Berry," *New York Times* reviewer A. O. Scott wrote, "proves herself to be an actress of impressive courage and insight. . . . Leticia is a character who could have been simplified, turned into a one-dimensional

In *Monster's Ball* (2001), Halle starred opposite Billy Bob Thornton. Her portrayal of the tough but vulnerable Leticia Musgrove earned Halle an Oscar.

victim or a saint. Ms. Berry emphasizes the character's temper, and also the vulnerability beneath her toughness."

"In *Monster's Ball*," biographer Christopher John Farley wrote, "Halle Berry gives a performance for the ages." Her peers in the Academy of Motion Picture Arts and Sciences agreed. For her portrayal of Leticia Musgrove, Halle won the Best Actress Oscar.

Rollercoaster

Halle seemed to be on a roll. The next few years turned out to be more like a rollercoaster.

After *Monster's Ball*, Halle costarred with Pierce Brosnan in *Die Another Day* (2002). It was the 20th installment in one of Hollywood's best-known and most-successful movie franchises: the James Bond movies. Bond is a British spy with a penchant for beautiful woman. In *Die Another Day*, Halle Berry broke new ground, becoming the first African American "Bond girl." She played Jinx, an American secret agent.

> **READ MORE**
> The fictional character James Bond has been entertaining readers and moviegoers for more than 50 years. Turn to page 49 to learn more about Bond's creator and about the history of the series.

In one scene from the movie, James Bond asks Jinx, "Do you believe in bad luck?" She responds, "Let's just say my relationships don't seem to last." The onscreen exchange could aptly describe Halle Berry's personal life. In 2003, within a year of the release of *Die Another Day*, she and Eric Benét had separated. Rumors circulated that Benét had repeatedly cheated on Halle. She filed for divorce in 2004.

That wasn't a banner year for her professionally, either. Halle played the lead role in *Catwoman*, a film that bombed at the box office and was ridiculed by the critics. For her work in the film, Halle was saddled with a Razzie Award as Worst Actress. The Golden Raspberry Awards, or Razzies, mock the worst films and performances of the previous year. The 2004 Razzies were given out at the Ivar Theatre in Los Angeles on February 26, 2005. Halle surprised and delighted the audience by showing up in person to accept her Razzie. With her Oscar statuette in one hand and her Razzie (a small golden raspberry) in the other, Halle launched into an acceptance speech in which she poked fun at her own emotional acceptance speech at the 2002 Academy Awards. "It was just what my career needed—I was at the top and now I'm at the bottom," she said. Clearly this was an actress who had learned not to take herself too seriously.

> **READ MORE**
>
> Actors dream of hearing their name follow the words "And the winner is . . ."—but not at the Razzie Awards. See page 50 for more information about the awards reserved for film's worst.

CHAPTER FIVE

A NEW CHAPTER

By 2006, as she approached her 40th birthday, Halle Berry could take satisfaction in all she had accomplished. She was a genuine Hollywood superstar. She was recognized by film critics and by her peers as a fine actress. She was also very popular with the moviegoing public and could command a huge salary—as much as $14 million per film.

Quietly, Halle was also putting her fame and fortune to use in helping people who weren't quite so fortunate. Among her favorite charities were organizations focusing on women and children. In 2002 Halle was honored by the Make-A-Wish Foundation as its celebrity wish-granter of the year. The Make-A-Wish Foundation helps terminally ill children. Halle was also a major supporter of the Jenesse Center, which helps women and children who are victims of domestic violence. Other causes Halle has helped include diabetes research, women's cancer research, and the Afghanistan Relief Organization, which

> **READ MORE**
> For information about the Make-A-Wish Foundation, one of Halle Berry's favorite charities, see page 51.

Halle Berry arrives at a benefit gala for the Make-A-Wish Foundation, Century City, California, October 26, 2002. Halle has been a major supporter of the organization, which grants the wishes of children with life-threatening illnesses.

provides food, medicine, and educational supplies to that war-torn country.

Motherhood

In 2006 Halle reprised her role as Storm in *X-Men: The Last Stand*, the third installment of the series (*X2*, the second X-Men movie, had come out three years earlier). Two films in 2007 had her in more serious roles. In *Perfect Stranger*, a mystery/thriller with Bruce Willis, she played a journalist who investigates the murder of a childhood friend. In *Things We Lost in the Fire*, Halle starred as Audrey Burke, a woman whose husband has just died tragically. Audrey invites his best friend, Jerry, a recovering heroin addict played by Benicio Del Toro, to live in her garage because she knows that is what her husband would have wanted. Audrey tries to help her houseguest stay clean as she struggles to raise her two young children on her own. Critics generally liked *Things We Lost in the Fire* and found Halle's performance as the grieving widow and mother believable.

This was most likely due to Halle's intense efforts to get inside the head of her character. "Every day," she would later say, "I dealt with the character as a mother and thinking as a mother." And this made Halle realize something about herself: she, too, wanted to be a mother.

In November 2005 Halle had met Gabriel Aubry, a French Canadian model and restaurant owner, at a photo shoot. After her painful breakup with Eric Benét, she wasn't looking for another relationship. "I thought it would be OK to be on my own," she recalled. Yet she found herself drawn to Aubrey, in part because he was different from other men she had known. "He was disarmingly sweet and caring and different," Halle said. "In the past I've been attracted to big personalities. Gabriel was shy. He hardly talked to me at first. I had to work at this a little."

A New Chapter | 39

The actress with boyfriend Gabriel Aubry, May 2007. She met the French Canadian model at a 2005 photo shoot.

Halle Berry

A visibly pregnant Halle Berry at the 19th Annual Palm Springs International Film Festival Awards, Palm Springs, California, January 5, 2008. In March, Halle gave birth to a daughter, Nahla Ariela Aubry.

A New Chapter

As their relationship blossomed and as she immersed herself in the character of Audrey Burke, Halle began to think about having children. "I hope that a baby finds me soon," she told *People* magazine in April 2007, the same month she was awarded a star on Hollywood's celebrated Walk of Fame. Halle wouldn't have to wait long for a baby. In September 2007, she announced that she was pregnant. And on March 16, 2008, she and Gabriel Aubry welcomed a daughter, Nahla Ariela Aubry.

"Once you meet a roadblock and overcome it," Halle Berry once noted, "you don't get scared by them anymore." The actress has encountered many obstacles, yet through hard work, determination, and perseverance she has risen to the top of her profession.

Looking to the Future

As 2008 came to a close, Halle had at least four film projects in various stages of production. She referred to this time in her life as the "second chapter," and she said she hoped to continually move forward personally as well as professionally.

Halle's second chapter may or may not include another Academy Award–winning performance. Life, which has sent Halle so many obstacles and so much heartbreak, may hold more adversity for her. But Halle Maria Berry seems ready to deal with whatever comes her way. "At times I thought things were going to break me," she once noted. "But somehow, through those experiences, this optimistic person evolved. Now I know nothing will break me."

CROSS-CURRENTS

Historic Evening

The 74th Academy Awards ceremony, held on March 24, 2002, turned out to be a historic night for African American performers. In addition to Halle Berry's Best Actress win—the first ever for a black woman—another African American garnered Best Actor honors. Denzel Washington took home the Oscar for his portrayal of a corrupt police officer in *Training Day*. This was just the second time a black performer in a leading role was awarded the Oscar. Washington had been nominated twice before in the Best Actor category—for his role as boxer Rubin Carter in *The Hurricane* (1999) and for the title role in 1992's *Malcolm X*, about the murdered Nation of Islam leader. Washington had also won an Oscar in the Best Supporting Actor category, for his role as a black soldier in the Civil War film *Glory* (1989). In addition, he was nominated for but did not win Best Supporting Actor honors for his portrayal of South African civil rights activist Steve Biko in *Cry Freedom* (1987).

African Americans shone at the 74th Academy Awards. Above: Best Actor recipient Denzel Washington and Best Actress winner Halle Berry. Opposite page: Sidney Poitier holds his special Oscar for lifetime achievement.

CROSS-CURRENTS

The 74th Academy Awards also celebrated the work of another well-known African American actor: Sidney Poitier. In 1964 Poitier became the first African American to win an Oscar in the Best Actor category, for his portrayal of a handyman in *Lilies of the Field*. Poitier had earlier received a Best Actor nomination for 1958's *The Defiant Ones*, in which he played an escaped convict shackled to a racist white prisoner. Other notable films in which he starred include *Porgy and Bess* (1959), *A Raisin in the Sun* (1961), *A Patch of Blue* (1965), *Guess Who's Coming to Dinner* (1967), and *In the Heat of the Night* (1967). At the 74th Academy Awards, the board of governors of the Academy of Motion Picture Arts and Sciences honored Poitier with a special Oscar for lifetime achievement. The award cited his "extraordinary performances and unique presence on the screen" as well as his representation of the motion picture industry "with dignity, style and intelligence."

CROSS-CURRENTS

Dorothy Dandridge

Dorothy Jean Dandridge was born in Cleveland, Ohio, in 1922. Her mother, Ruby Dandridge, was an entertainer who prodded Dorothy and her sister, Vivian, into performing from young ages. As a 12-year-old Dorothy had a small, uncredited role in the 1935 Little Rascals movie *Teacher's Beau*. Bit parts in various movies followed. By the late 1930s Dorothy had dropped out of high school to perform in nightclubs with the Dandridge Sisters. The singing trio consisted of Dorothy, her sister, and Etta James, who would go on to enjoy a long and successful musical career.

In 1942 Dorothy Dandridge married Harold Nicholas, a dancer she had met the year before. For the rest of the decade, Dandridge largely put her career on hold, to run the household and to care for her severely developmentally disabled daughter, Harolyn, born in 1943. But the marriage was unhappy.

In the early 1950s, after divorcing Nicholas, Dandridge resumed her career. She won international acclaim as a nightclub singer. But Dandridge wasn't allowed to stay overnight in many of the hotels and resorts in the United States where she performed. Nor was she allowed to ride on the elevators, swim in the pools, or use the restrooms that white patrons used.

Dorothy Dandridge in *Island in the Sun* (1957).

Dandridge's success as a singer revived her movie career. In 1953 she starred opposite Harry Belafonte in *Bright Road*. The following year brought her best-known role: as the title character in *Carmen Jones*. The musical—an adaptation of the famous opera *Carmen*—had a great cast of African American performers, including Belafonte, Pearl Bailey, and Diahann Carroll. But it was Dandridge who stood out, as a seductive woman who lures a decent soldier away from his fiancée—and from the army—only to dump him later for a boxer. Dandridge's performance won her an Academy Award nomination for Best Actress in a Leading Role, the first ever for an African American. In November 1954, *Life* magazine put her on its cover—another first for an African American woman.

Dandridge seemed to have a bright future in Hollywood. Yet even with her Academy Award nomination, she found it difficult to get other leading roles because of her race.

Her personal life was tumultuous. She had a series of unhappy relationships, including several with white men—drawing the strong disapproval of the Hollywood filmmaking community. In 1959 Dandridge married a white restaurant owner, but he was physically abusive and took much of her money. They were divorced within a few years. Dandridge declared bankruptcy in 1963.

With her career and personal life in tatters, Dandridge began to drink excessively. On September 8, 1965, she died of an overdose of prescription medication, age 42.

CROSS-CURRENTS

Supporting Roles

While Halle Berry was, as of 2008, the only African American to take home an Oscar for Best Actress in a Leading Role, three black performers had won Best Supporting Actress honors. The first was Hattie McDaniel, who won for her role as Mammy, the sharp-tongued nurse and house slave to Scarlett O'Hara in the 1939 Civil War–era epic *Gone with the Wind*. McDaniel was the first African American to be nominated for an Academy Award in any category.

A half century would pass before another black woman won an Oscar. In 1991 Whoopi Goldberg took home Best Supporting Actress honors for her role in *Ghost* (1990). The film was a romantic fantasy, but Goldberg brought her considerable comedic talents to her portrayal of Oda Mae Brown, a fake psychic medium who one day actually does hear a ghost. Five years before winning her Oscar, Goldberg had been nominated for Best Supporting Actress for her work in *The Color Purple*, an adaptation of the Alice Walker novel.

Jennifer Hudson first entered the spotlight as a singer, on the 2004 season of *American Idol*. But Hudson demonstrated her acting ability in *Dreamgirls* (2006). Although it was her first film, Hudson won an Oscar as Best Supporting Actress.

Singer and actress Jennifer Hudson. Hudson won a Best Supporting Actress Oscar in her first film, the 2006 musical drama *Dreamgirls*.

CROSS-CURRENTS

Diabetes

Diabetes is a medical disorder in which the body cannot produce or use insulin, a hormone that regulates glucose (sugar) in the bloodstream. Insulin takes glucose from the blood into the body's cells, where the glucose is broken down and converted into energy. When the process is disrupted, serious medical conditions may result. These include damage to the eyes, kidneys, nerves, or heart. In extreme cases, diabetes can lead to amputation of the lower limbs and other life-threatening health issues. While it can affect anyone, diabetes is more common among the elderly and among blacks, Latinos, Native Americans, and people of Asian/Pacific islander ancestry.

There are two types of diabetes. Type 1, formerly called juvenile diabetes, is the less common. Most frequently diagnosed in children and young adults, type 1 diabetes is characterized by an inability of the body to produce any insulin. In type 2 diabetes, which is generally diagnosed in adults (often after age 45), the body either doesn't produce enough insulin or the cells cannot use insulin properly.

Though serious, diabetes can be managed. People with the disease must check their blood glucose levels on a regular basis and give themselves insulin shots as necessary. They should watch their diet, get enough exercise, avoid smoking and drinking excessive amounts of alcohol, and learn to manage stress. By taking these steps, diabetics can live long and healthy lives.

A young diabetic learns how to check her sugar levels with a blood glucose meter.

CROSS-CURRENTS

The Golden Globes

The Oscar may be the American film industry's most recognizable symbol of excellence. But another prestigious awards ceremony takes place each year in Hollywood as well: the Golden Globes.

Sponsored by the Hollywood Foreign Press Association (HFPA), the Golden Globes date to the 1940s. In 1944 a best actor, a best actress, and a best film were selected, with the winners each receiving a scroll. The next year the distinctive trophy that is awarded today was created. It consists of a gold-colored globe atop a pedestal and circled by movie film.

For the first decade of the award's existence, Golden Globes were given only for work in motion pictures. In 1955, however, the HFPA began honoring outstanding work in television as well. Today Golden Globes are awarded in 14 film and 11 television categories.

The Golden Globes are given in January, a month before the Academy Awards. Many Hollywood observers consider the Golden Globes a good predictor of who is likely to win an Oscar.

Halle Berry plants a kiss on her Golden Globe statue, January 23, 2000. She won for Best Performance by an Actress in a Mini-Series or Movie Made for TV, for *Introducing Dorothy Dandridge*.

CROSS-CURRENTS

Agent 007

James Bond, the fictional British secret agent designated 007, was the creation of a real British intelligence officer. Ian Fleming, born in 1908, served in British naval intelligence during World War II. He also supervised a special group of British commandos who carried out dangerous missions behind German lines.

After the war, Fleming devoted himself to writing, dividing his time between England and Jamaica. In 1953 he introduced the character of James Bond in the novel *Casino Royale*. The book was a popular success, and Fleming cranked out another Bond novel every year until his death, from a heart attack, in 1964. Other writers soon began producing James Bond stories.

In 1962 agent 007 made the transition from printed page to movie screen, with *Dr. No*. More than 20 films later, with the release of *Quantum of Solace* (2008), the Bond movie franchise was still going strong.

The enduring appeal of the series is attributable largely to the character Ian Fleming created. James Bond is fearless, suave, and unflappable as he travels the globe foiling the plots of cunning villains and making the acquaintance of beautiful women.

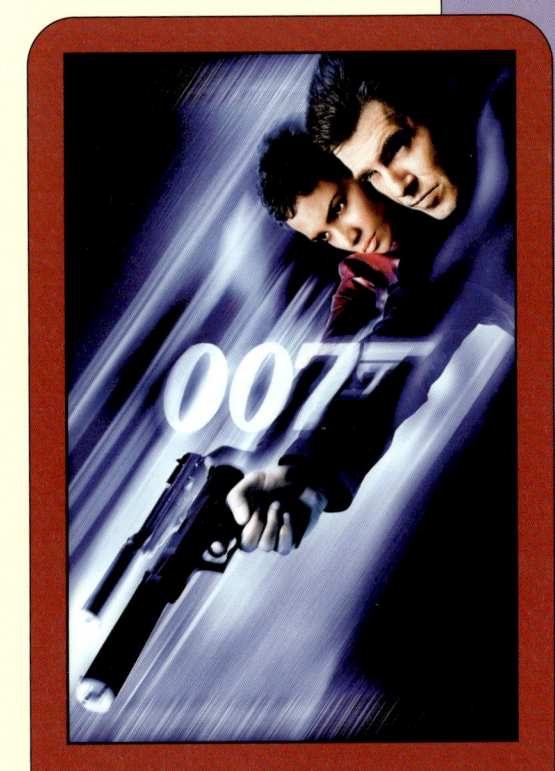

Halle Berry and Pierce Brosnan grace this movie poster for *Die Another Day*. Halle broke new ground in the 2002 James Bond thriller, becoming the first African American "Bond girl" in the long history of the 007 franchise.

CROSS-CURRENTS

An Award Nobody Wants

The Golden Raspberry Awards, or Razzies, are awarded annually for the year's worst performances in film. Some of the categories are negative versions of the Academy Awards, such as Worst Picture, Worst Actor and Actress, and Worst Supporting Actor and Actress. Other categories have no Oscar equivalent. These include Worst Screen Couple and Worst Remake or Rip-off.

The purpose of the Razzies—founded in 1980 by copywriter and publicist John Wilson—is to parody, or poke fun at, Hollywood and the Academy Awards. Winners receive a gold-painted plastic raspberry.

Some big-name stars have been tapped for Razzies. Among the actors and actresses to win Academy Awards as well as Razzies are Marlon Brando, Roberto Benigni, Halle Bery, Faye Dunaway, Charlton Heston, Liza Minelli, and Laurence Olivier. Sylvester Stallone owns the dubious distinction of having amassed the most Razzie nominations—30—along with 10 wins. Madonna comes in second, with 15 nominations and several wins for Worst Actress. The 2003 box office bomb *Gigli* made Razzie history by sweeping the top awards: Worst Picture, Worst Director (Martin Brest), Worst Screenplay (Brest) Worst Actor (Ben Affleck), and Worst Actress (Jennifer Lopez).

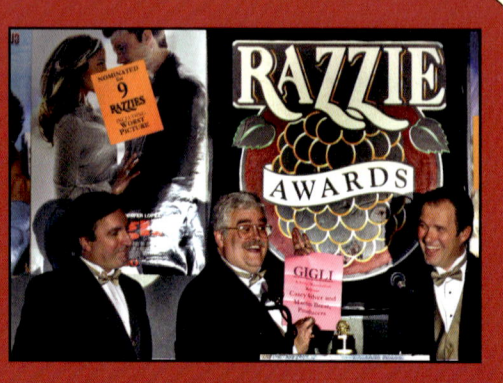

Gigli wins the Razzie as 2003's worst picture at the 24th Annual Golden Raspberry Awards, February 28, 2004.

CROSS-CURRENTS

The Make-A-Wish Foundation

The Make-A-Wish Foundation is a charitable organization that grants the wishes of children with life-threatening medical conditions. The foundation's origins date to 1980, when law enforcement officers in Arizona learned that seven-year-old leukemia patient Christopher Greicius had always wanted to be a policeman. The officers gave the boy a tour in a police helicopter, had a uniform made for him, showed him how to ride a motorcycle, and swore him in as an honorary patrolman. Chris passed away shortly afterward, but the roots of the Make-A-Wish Foundation were planted.

Since then the foundation has helped more that 170,000 seriously ill children worldwide fulfill their dreams. To be eligible, a child must be between the ages of $2\frac{1}{2}$ and 18, and his or doctor must determine that carrying out the wish won't worsen the child's condition.

Although the average cost of fulfilling a wish was, as of August 2005, more than $6,000, the families of wish recipients don't have to pay anything. The Make-A-Wish Foundation pays expenses through donations and relies on the help of more than 25,000 volunteers, including celebrities such as Halle Berry.

Kaden Graham looks out the cockpit of a jetliner at Seattle-Tacoma International Airport before a flight to Disneyland. The five-year-old's dream trip was made possible by the Make-A-Wish Foundation.

Chronology

1966: Halle Maria Berry is born on August 14 in Cleveland, Ohio, to Judith and Jerome Berry.

1970: Jerome Berry abandons the family.

1976: Halle's parents attempt to reconcile, but they split up for good following Jerome Berry's physical abuse.

1985: Halle is crowned Miss Teen All American.

1986: Is first runner-up in Miss USA beauty pageant.

1989: Lands television role on *Living Dolls*.

1991: Lands first movie role, playing a drug addict in Spike Lee's *Jungle Fever*.

1992: Marries baseball star David Justice.

1996: Files for divorces from Justice; the divorce becomes finalized the following year.

1999: Gains critical acclaim as actress and producer of *Introducing Dorothy Dandridge*.

2000: Plays the mutant Storm in the blockbuster movie *X-Men*; involved in a hit-and-run car accident.

Chronology

2001: Plays Leticia Musgrove in *Monster's Ball*; marries second husband, Eric Benét.

2002: Wins historic Best Actress Academy Award for role in *Monster's Ball*; plays first African American "Bond girl" in *Die Another Day*.

2004: Files for divorce from Eric Benét.

2005: Divorce from Benét becomes final; meets Canadian model Gabriel Aubry on a photo shoot.

2006: Stars in third X-Men movie.

2008: Gives birth to a daughter, Nahla Ariela Aubry.

Accomplishments & Awards

Selected Filmography

Jungle Fever (1991)

Strictly Business (1991)

The Last Boy Scout (1991)

Boomerang (1992)

Father Hood (1993)

The Program (1993)

The Flintstones (1994)

Losing Isaiah (1995)

Executive Decision (1996)

Race the Sun (1996)

The Rich Man's Wife (1996)

*B*A*P*S* (1997)

Bulworth (1998)

Why Do Fools Fall in Love (1998)

Introducing Dorothy Dandridge (1999) (TV)

X-Men (2000)

Swordfish (2001)

Monster's Ball (2001)

Die Another Day (2002)

X2 (2003)

Gothika (2003)

Catwoman (2004)

Their Eyes Were Watching God (2005) (TV)

Robots (2005) (voice)

X-Men: The Last Stand (2006)

Perfect Stranger (2007)

Things We Lost in the Fire (2007)

Selected Awards

Academy Award

Best Actress in a Leading Role, for *Monster's Ball* (2002)

Emmy Award

Outstanding Lead Actress in a Miniseries or a Movie, for *Introducing Dorothy Dandridge* (2000)

Golden Globe Award

Best Performance by an Actress in a Mini-Series or Motion Picture Made for TV, for *Introducing Dorothy Dandridge* (2000)

Screen Actors Guild Awards

Outstanding Performance by a Female Actor in a Television Movie or Miniseries, for *Introducing Dorothy Dandridge* (2000)

Outstanding Performance by a Female Actor in a Leading Role, for *Monster's Ball* (2002)

Further Reading

Banting, Erinn. *Halle Berry (Great African American Women)*. New York: Weigl Publishers, 2005.

Farley, Christopher John. *Introducing Halle Berry*. New York: Pocket Books, 2002.

Sanello, Frank. *Halle Berry: A Stormy Life*. London: Virgin Publishing, 2004.

Internet Resources

http://www.hallewood.com/

Halle Berry's official Web site contains her biography, news, charity information, and more.

http://www.imdb.com/name/nm0000932/

The page, from the Internet Movie Database, lists Halle Berry's film and television credits and includes a short biography.

http://www.diabetes.org

The Web site of the American Diabetes Association provides a wide range of helpful information about diabetes, how it is diagnosed, and how it is treated.

Publisher's Note: The Web sites listed on this page were active at the time of publication. The publisher is not responsible for Web sites that have changed their address or discontinued operation since the date of publication. The publisher reviews and updates the Web sites each time the book is reprinted.

Glossary

audition—an opportunity for an actor to win a role in a play or movie.

biracial—consisting of, representing, or combining members of two separate races.

diabetes—a serious medical condition in which the body is unable to produce sufficient insulin to regulate blood sugar (glucose) levels.

discrimination—unfair or prejudiced treatment of a person based on the racial, ethnic, or other group to which that person belongs.

franchise—the right or license granted by a company to an individual or group to market its products or services.

insulin—a hormone that regulates the metabolism of glucose and other nutrients.

prestigious—having a high reputation; honored; esteemed.

producer—the person who is responsible for raising money to make a movie, and for hiring people to work on the film.

racism—hatred or intolerance of another race or other races, or a belief that one race is superior to another.

tabloid—a publication or program that focuses on gossip or scandalous news.

Chapter Notes

p. 6: "This moment is so much . . ." "Halle Berry 2002 Oscar Acceptance Address for Best Actress," American Rhetoric Online Speech Bank. http://www.americanrhetoric.com/speeches/halleberryoscarspeech.htm

p. 10: "It felt like validation," Laura B. Randolph, "Halle Berry: On How She Found Dorothy Dandridge's Spirit—And Finally Healed Her Own," *Ebony*, August 1999, p. 91.

p. 13: "He beat my mom . . ." Dana Kennedy, "Oscar Films: Halle Berry, Bruised and Beautiful, Is on a Mission," *New York Times*, March 10, 2002.

p. 15: "She taught me when . . ." Ibid.

p. 15: "I never did high-school plays . . ." Diane Clehane, "Halle's Comet," *Biography*, vol. 5, issue 1 (January 2001): 60.

p. 16: "I was the head cheerleader . . ." Lynn Hirschberg, "The Beautiful and Damned," *New York Times*, December 23, 2001.

p. 17: "Pageants teach you . . ." Jill Gerston, "Film; The Prom's Co-Queen Finally Gets Her Revenge," *New York Times*, March 12, 1995. http://query.nytimes.com/gst/fullpage.html?res=990CE4DC1431F931A25750C0A963958260

p. 19: "It took five years . . . " Suzanne Ely, "Halle Berry: Her Secret Source of Strength," *Redbook*, vol. 200, issue 3 (March 1, 2003): 130.

p. 20: "I liked that part better . . ." Hirschberg, "The Beautiful and Damned."

p. 21: "I went to a crack house . . ." Ely, "Her Secret Source."

p. 22: "Some [film] executive . . ." Kennedy, "Halle Berry, Bruised and Beautiful."

p. 22: "I want the same shot . . ." Gerston, "The Prom's Co-Queen."

p. 24: "Frankly, we wondered . . ." Ibid.

p. 24: "With every take . . ." Ibid.

p. 24: "Ms. Berry is the most . . ." Janet Maslin, "Film Review; A Little Boy and a Plot Worthy of Solomon," *New York Times,* March 17, 1995. http://movies.nytimes.com/movie/review?res=990CE4D81130F934A25750C0A963958260

p. 24: "I wasn't good . . ." Hirschberg, "The Beautiful and Damned."

p. 26: "I had to track . . ." Bebe Moore Campbell, "Halle Berry the Inside Story," *Essence,* vol. 27, issue 6 (October 1996): 70.

p. 27: "It's a comedy . . ." Laura B. Randolph, "Halle Berry—Film Star," *Ebony* (March 1997). http://findarticles.com/p/articles/mi_m1077/is_/ai_19201532?tag=artBody;col1

p. 30: "People I thought . . ." Laura Randolph Lancaster, "Halle Berry: On Her Public Troubles, Private Joys & Sudden Desire for a Baby," *Ebony* (August 2000).

p. 30: "As the weeks went by . . ." Ibid.

p. 32: "The mutants face . . ." Ibid.

p. 32: "We met for lunch . . ." Jim Calio, "Halle's Moment," *Good Housekeeping,* vol. 235, issue 2 (August 2002): 98.

Chapter Notes

p. 32: "Of course, she was . . ." Ibid.

p. 33: "Ms. Berry proves herself . . ." A. O. Scott, "Film Review; Courtesy and Decency Play Sneaky with a Tough Guy," *New York Times*, December 26, 2001. http://movies.nytimes.com/movie/review?res=9C07EED81531F935A15751C1A9679C8B63

p. 34: "In *Monster's Ball* . . ." Christopher John Farley, *Introducing Halle Berry* (New York: Pocket Books, 2002), p. 204.

p. 35: "It was just what my career . . ." Helen Bushby, "Berry Gets Worst Actress Razzie," BBC News online, February 27, 2005. http://news.bbc.co.uk/2/hi/entertainment/4301783.stm

p. 38: "Every day I dealt . . ." Associated Press, "Halle Berry Talks Pregnancy, Plans for More," MSNBC, October 2, 2007. http://www.msnbc.msn.com/id/21102461

p. 38: "I thought it would be OK . . ." Tim Allis, "The Rise and Shine of Halle Berry," *InStyle* (April 2007).

p. 38: "He was disarmingly . . ." Ibid.

p. 41: "I hope that a baby . . ." Karen S. Schneider et al., "Halle's Joy!" *People* (September 17, 2007).

p. 41: "Once you meet a roadblock . . ." "Halle Berry: Strictly Business About Show Business," *Ebony* (February 1992).

p. 41: "At times I thought things . . ." Allis, "Rise and Shine."

p. 43: "extraordinary performances . . ." Associated Press, "Poitier to Get Honorary Oscar," chicagotribune.com, January 24, 2002. http://www.chicagotribune.com/business/bal-artslife-winner-academy-poitier24,0,143006.story

Index

Academy Awards, 6–8, 9–10, *11*, 12, 34, 42
Afghanistan Relief Organization, 36, 38
Aubry, Gabriel, 38, *39*, 41
Aubry, Nahla Ariela, 41

B*A*P*S, 26–27
Bassett, Angela, 6
Beatty, Warren, 27
beauty pageants, 17
Bedford High School (Cleveland), 16
Benét, Eric, 28, 30–31, 34
Benét, India, 31
Berry, Halle
  and African American role models, 6–8
  awards, 6–8, 10, *11*, 12, 17, 28, 34, 35, 41, 42, *48*, 50, 55
  beauty pageants, 17
  birth and family, 13–14
  charity work, 36–37. *See also* Make-A-Wish Foundation
  childhood interests, 15–17
  daughter (adopted), 31
  and David Justice, 24–26
  and diabetes, 19
  and directors worked for, 20, 21, 24
  and domestic abuse, 13, 24, 36
  and Dorothy Dandridge connection, 10–11, 12
  education, 15–17
  and Eric Benét, 28, 30–31
  fear of abandonment, 14, 26, 30
  and female costars, *18*, *23*, 24
  and film roles, 10, 12, 20–22, 23–24, 26–27, *29*, 31–35, 38, *49*
  hit-and-run accident, 28, 30
  identity confusion, 14–15, 16
  and male costars, 20, 22, 27, 32, 33, 34, 38, *49*
  marriages, 24–26, 31, 34
  and motherhood, 38, *40*, 41
  overcoming adversity, 41
  prejudices against her beauty, 20, *21*, 22, 24, 32
  and producers worked for, 32
  recovery from divorce, 26–27
  and romantic interests, 24, 28, 30–31, 38–39
  and TV roles, *18*, 19
  See also racial prejudices
Berry, Heidi (sister), 14
Berry, Jerome (father), 13–14, 26
Brosnan, Pierce, 34, *49*
Bulworth, 27

Carroll, Diahann, 6, 12, 45
Catwoman, 34–35
Cirrincione, Vincent, 17, 19, 22
civil rights movement, 8, 9
Cleveland, Ohio, 13, *15*, 16
Crowe, Russell, 6
Cuyahoga Community College (Cleveland), 16

Dandridge, Dorothy, 6, 8–9, 10, 12, 44–45
Daniels, Lee, 32
Del Toro, Benicio, 38
Dench, Judi, 6
diabetes, 19, 47, 57
Die Another Day, 34

Elliott, Alison, *18*
Emmy Awards, 12
Executive Decision, 22

Numbers in ***bold italics*** refer to captions.

Index

The Flintstones, 22
Fox, Vivica, 6

Goldberg, Whoopi, 10, 46
Golden Globe Awards, 12, 28, 48
Gyllenhaal, Stephen, 24

Hawkins, Judith (mother), 13–14, 26
Hollywood Walk of Fame, 41
Horne, Lena, 6, 12
Hudson, Jennifer, 46

Introducing Dorothy Dandridge, 10, 12, 27, 28, **29**
Ivar Theatre, 35

Jackson, Samuel L., 20
James Bond movies, 34, 49
Jenesse Center, 36
Jim Crow laws, 8, 9
Jungle Fever, 20–22, 24
Justice, David, 24–26

Kidman, Nicole, 6
Knots Landing, 19
Kodak Theatre, 6

Lange, Jessica, **23**, 24
Lansing, Sherry, 24
The Last Boy Scout, 22
Lee, Spike, 20, 21
Learned, Michael, **18**, 19
Living Dolls, **18**, 19
Losing Isaiah, 23–24

Make-A-Wish Foundation, 36, 37, 51
McDaniel, Hattie, 46
Monster's Ball, 12, 32–34

Perfect Stranger, 38
Pinkett, Jada, 6
Poitier, Sidney, 43

racial prejudices, 8, 9, 12, 13, 14–16, 22, 42–43, 44
Razzie Awards, 35, 50
Remini, Leah, **18**

Spacek, Sissy, 6
Swordfish, 12

Things We Lost in the Fire, 38
Thornton, Billy Bob, 32, **33**
Tucker, Deborah, **18**
type 2 diabetes, 19, 47

Washington, Denzel, 10, 42
Wayans, Damon, 22
Willis, Bruce, 22, 38

X-Men, 12, 31–32
X-Men: The Last Stand, 38

Zellweger, Renée, 6

Photo Credits

- 7: John McCoy/WireImage/Getty Images
- 9: Hulton Archive/Getty Images
- 11: Frank Micelotta/Stringer/Getty Images
- 14: Albert C. Ortega/WireImage/Getty Images
- 15: Used under license from Shutterstock, Inc.
- 16: Seth Poppel Yearbook Library
- 18: Warner Bros/ABC-TV/The Kobal Collection
- 21: Universal/The Kobal Collection/Lee, David
- 23: Paramount/The Kobal Collection
- 25: Jeff Kravitz/FilmMagic/Getty Images
- 29: Esparza/Katz Prod/The Kobal Collection/Zahedi, Firooz
- 31: Randall Michelson Archive/WireImage/Getty Images
- 33: Lions Gate/The Kobal Collection/Bulliard, Jeanne Louise
- 37: Robert Mora/Getty Images
- 39: Charley Gallay/Stringer/Getty Images
- 40: Gregg DeGuire/WireImage/Getty Images
- 41: Jeffrey Mayer/WireImage/Getty Images
- 42: Lee Celano/AFP/Getty Images
- 43: Frank Micelotta/Stringer/Getty Images
- 44: Hulton Archive/Getty Images
- 46: Used under license from Shutterstock, Inc.
- 47: Used under license from Shutterstock, Inc.
- 48: Vince Bucci/AFP/Getty Images
- 49: Danjaq/EON/UA/The Kobal Collection
- 50: The Associated Press
- 51: 2008 The Associated Press

Cover Images
Main Image: Kevin Winter/Getty Images
Top Inset: Anthony Harvey/Getty Images
Bottom Inset: Mark Davis/Getty Images

About the Author

MAURENE J. HINDS is a freelance writer and instructor. She has written several books for young readers. She holds an MFA in Writing for Children and Young Adults from Vermont College.